For Janet

Enjoy Aku!

Peace
Joy
Love

Ashley Bryan
'79

BOOKS BY ASHLEY BRYAN

The Ox of the Wonderful Horns and Other African Folktales
Walk Together Children: Black American Spirituals
The Adventures of Aku

The Adventures of
Aku

Love

Ashley Bryan

The Adventures of
Aku

or

*How it came about that we
shall always see Okra the cat
lying on a velvet cushion,
while Okraman the dog sleeps
among the ashes.*

RETOLD AND ILLUSTRATED BY

ASHLEY BRYAN

Atheneum · New York

1976

Library of Congress Cataloging in Publication Data
Bryan, Ashley. The Adventures of Aku.
SUMMARY: When sent to retrieve their master's magic ring
from Spider Ananse, Okra the cat and Okraman the dog
prove their true worth.
[1. Folklore—Africa]   I. Title.
PZ8.1.B838Ad   398.2′452   75-44245
ISBN 0-689-30519-2

Published simultaneously in Canada by
McClelland & Stewart, Ltd.
Printed in the United States of America by
Connecticut Printers, Hartford, Connecticut
Bound by A. Horowitz and Son
Fairfield, New Jersey
Designed by Ashley Bryan and Mary M. Ahern
First Edition

For Ernestine and Kenneth Haskins

ASHANTI PROVERB:
No one knows the story of tomorrow's dawn.

The Adventures of
Aku

A long time ago

Cat and Dog lived among people as brothers. They shared equally in all things wherever they lived whether it was in hut, house or hovel. Each had his own mat to sleep upon, and each had his own dish for dinner. Indeed, in those days they were treated as children.

Then how did it come about that Cat eats from a dish while Dog eats from the floor? That Cat and Dog now hardly get along at all, and that we always see Cat lying on a velvet cushion while Dog sleeps on the ashes?

Hmm . . . that is a question within a question. And the answer is a story within a story. It is like Spider Ananse's famous box that plays a part in this tale.

Open the outer box and within lies another. Each locked box holds a smaller box. Finally, unlock the smallest box of all. There Spider has hidden the Ring of All Wishes.

Whoever finds a way to the innermost box—and that takes wit—wins the treasure. And whoever listens to this story within a story—and that takes time—learns at the

3

end why it is that we always see Cat lying on a velvet cushion while Dog sleeps among the ashes.

LET US start with the outer box, which is to say, at the beginning and work our way to the innermost box, which is to say, to the end.

By the Forest of Mampon, on the edge of a village, there lived a woman named Onyema.

Onyema was well along in years and had been unlucky in life. She had lost her children soon after birth and now even her husband had died. Onyema was alone.

She spent many hours sitting beside the lily pond in her garden, watching the reflection of her hut and fruit trees in the water.

"Everything's upside down," she thought, "and that's just how I feel without even a child for company."

The villagers passed Onyema's compound on their way to the hills to consult the Lesser Gods, known as the Abosom. They'd greet Onyema, admire her garden and the lily pond, then continue on.

One noon, Onyema sat longing and dozing by the pond until she fell asleep.

In a dream she saw her mango tree bearing fruit. One fruit swelled and swelled till its weight snapped the branch. The huge fruit fell to the ground and broke open. The long seed cracked and a boy sprang out.

He leaped and laughed before Onyema. She was delighted with the child. When the boy came near, Onyema
reached out to touch him. He darted and disappeared
among the hills of the Abosom.

Onyema awoke thinking of the child and remember-
ing the Abosom. Bold as it seemed, she decided to consult
one of the Lesser Gods and ask for a son.

She picked three of the best fruits from her fruit trees
and folded them in a lily leaf.

She could not wait another day. So that night Onyema
climbed the side of the hill with the full moon.

"Yes, moon, come along and brighten the way. You've
played among the lily pads in my pond and you've heard
me. You know my wish already."

Onyema reached the abode of the Lesser God at the
top of the hill. She unfolded the lily leaf and spread out
the three fruits at the foot of a tree. The moonlight upon

the fruits made them glow like precious stones.

"I am alone," Onyema said when she felt the presence of the Lesser God. "I would like a child, a boy who will be strong and live at least as long as I have lived, and longer still. I've had no luck in rearing a child of my own."

The Lesser God spoke:

> *I accept the three fruits*
> *On the lily-pad dish.*
> *I promise, Onyema,*
> *To answer your wish.*
>
> *I've power to send soon*
> *A Spider-Story son.*
> *Until he's a youth*
> *He'll grow four years in one.*
>
> *Name the boy Aku.*
> *When the time's set*
> *He'll add to the family*
> *And land you in debt.*
>
> *Be patient and love him*
> *Though these pranks offend.*
> *His first foolish acts*
> *Will prove wise in the end.*

The moon brightened Onyema's path down the hill. The scent of herbs and flowers rose on the air. A bird stirred in its sleep as her step disturbed the still night. It sang drowsily "Su-wee, Su-wee" and went back to sleep. The world seemed charmed and wonderful to Onyema now that the Obosom had promised her a child.

When the Spider-Story child came, Onyema was prepared. She had woven a mat for the child's place in the hut. Outdoors, she had strung a mesh hammock between two trees by the pond.

The baby was alert and beautiful. Onyema was overjoyed. While she tended her garden, he lay in the hammock watching leaves and birds and listening to the frogs splashing among the lilies.

As the Lesser God had warned, Aku was not an ordinary child. It was not long before he tipped the hammock and touched the ground. Aku was soon playing in the garden, collecting the fallen fruit and catching frogs.

Onyema enjoyed every moment of Aku's swift growth. When he was small, she cradled him in her arms and sang to him.

As Aku grew older, they would sit together outdoors after dinner. Under the stars, as the embers of the last meal glowed, Onyema told Aku stories.

Aku loved Onyema's stories and songs. He repeated the tales to the frogs, and he sang the songs to the birds.

Onyema was proud of her Spider-Story son, and she never failed, when the full moon rose, to visit the Lesser God of the hills. Aku would carry her fruit offering of thanks.

During the first years these were Aku's only trips out of the compound. He had learned enough to know, however, that there was much more to be discovered in the wider world beyond his home.

Aku grew to be a handsome youth. Soon he was of an age when he could be helpful to his mother. And at that time, Onyema was glad to see that he now grew at the same rate as any other youth.

One day Aku watched Onyema, pestle in hand, pounding the plantain in the mortar. She sang as she worked. When the plaintain had been properly pounded, Onyema made it into fufu for dinner. A pot of relish simmered on the fire.

Onyema reached for the salt and emptied the last of it into the fufu.

"There," she said, "that is the last of the salt that I've just sprinkled into the fufu."

"Mother," said Aku, "let me go to buy the salt we need. You've told me tales of the Edge-of-the-Sea Country where salt is sought and bought. I'll go!"

"Aku, my son," said the Mother, "you've never gone anywhere alone." She stopped stirring the relish for the fufu and looked up at Aku. She saw he was now an able youth, ready for adventure. He could no longer be protected within the enclosure of her compound.

"Well," she said, "the road to the Edge-of-the-Sea Country is well traveled. You won't lose your way."

Aku kneeled down by the steaming pots and hugged his mother.

The

next morning, Onyema packed Aku's sack with fruit for the trip. She placed a small brass weight in one pan of her scale and measured out an equal weight of gold dust into the other pan.

"Here is an asuanu's weight in gold dust for the salt," she said.

Aku set out singing.

The villagers had never seen Aku outside of the confines of Onyema's compound. They were surprised to see him alone and made much of him as he strode by.

"I'm off to buy salt from the Edge-of-the-Sea Country," he said proudly.

The little children ran after Aku chanting:

> *Kwaku, Kwaku,*
> *Here comes Aku.*
> *Sell him salt*
> *To salt his fufu.*

They showed him the right road and ran back still singing: "Kwaku, Kwaku, . . ."

Aku walked along looking with curiosity and interest at everything he passed. When a plant intrigued him, he stopped to pluck it and put it in his sack.

"Mother knows plants," he thought. "I'll ask her about this one when I get home."

Aku saw trees that did not grow in his garden or in the nearby hills or at the edge of the forest that he could see from the compound. He saw animals and birds that had not come by his home.

So Aku proceeded slowly on his way, eating the fruit that his mother had packed for him. He had no trouble keeping to the well-traveled route to the Edge-of-the-Sea Country.

As he continued on, he met a man with a dog. Aku was delighted. His eyes opened wide with wonder when he saw how well the dog trotted beside the man.

"What a good friend to have," thought Aku. He forgot everything in his desire to have the dog.

"That is a wonderful dog," said Aku after greeting the man. "I would like to buy it."

"Oh no," said the man, "Okraman is always with me. Beside you could not afford to buy a dog like my Okraman."

"How much is it?" asked Aku.

"An asuanu's weight in gold dust."

"Ah! Good!" cried Aku. "That's just what I have." And he handed over the pouch of gold dust.

"Come Okraman," he called, "you're mine now. Come with me."

Aku turned back along the road that he had traveled. He returned home with the dog Okraman trotting beside him.

When Aku entered the hut, his mother looked up in surprise to see him back so soon.

"Aku! Back already?" she said. "You could not have reached the Edge-of-the-Sea Country."

"Sea Country? Oh no," said Aku. "Look mother! See what I was able to buy for us with the gold dust you gave me."

Aku called, and the dog came into the hut.

Onyema saw the dog and asked, "But what of the salt for the fufu?"

"Salt? Oh, the salt!" Only then did Aku remember what he had forgotten in his excitement over the dog.

"Ho!" said the mother. "That's just what the Obosom said I was to expect. Now we are really in for it if I do not go and get some salt myself."

So Onyema went and bought the salt herself.

AKU AND OKRAMAN the dog played together in the garden like brothers. Sometimes they left the compound to explore the nearby hills and forest. Eventually they knew where the best edible mushrooms grew, and Aku would collect them for his mother to use in the fufu relish.

Sometimes they went through their village on the way to visit Spider Ananse, who had become the Spider-Story child's best friend. Spider Ananse lived in a distant village. When Aku and Okraman went through their village, the little children clapped their hands and chanted:

Kwaku, Kwaku,
Here comes Okraman
Walking with Aku
Just like a human.

Indeed, at home Okraman the dog was treated like one of the family. At dinnertime, he sat between Aku and Onyema and ate from his own dish. And at night, he slept on his own sleeping mat in the hut, at Aku's side.

The full moon that greeted Okraman's arrival, waned. The days passed. Soon it was full moon time again.

Early one day, before the moon had faded out of the morning sky, Onyema sang as she pounded the last of the yams in the mortar. She had a good supply of salt on hand, but no more yams or plantain were left.

"Ho Aku!" she said. "Food goes faster with three to feed. Tonight we will sprinkle salt on the last of the fufu."

"Don't worry, Mother," said Aku. "Tomorrow morning Okraman and I will go to buy plantain and yams."

Even though the mother was now fond of the dog, she was afraid that Aku might throw away the money.

"And what if you 'burn' the gold dust again?" she asked.

Nevertheless, the next morning Onyema packed Aku's sack with fruits for the journey. She weighed out an asuanu-and-suru's weight of gold dust in her scales.

"Go to the village market of our friend Kwaku Ananse," she said. "He boasts that he is your best friend. Perhaps he will give you more than our gold dust's weight in vegetables."

Onyema placed the pouch of gold dust in the sack of fruits. Aku embraced his mother, then he and Okraman the dog set out.

Aku and Okraman shared the fruit as they traveled the road to market. Aku threw the fruit seeds along the side of the road.

"When these seeds grow up," he said to the dog, "there'll be fruit trees along the way to Kwaku Ananse's village. Then Mother won't have to pack fruit for us when we go marketing."

They went along until they met a man beside the road,

playing with a cat. He lifted the cat, turned it over and dropped it to the ground. The cat always landed on its feet.

"Oh," said Aku, "what a clever animal! See, Okraman, how it always falls on its feet!"

Okraman looked on with interest.

"I would like to own it," said Aku.

"What?" said the man. "Me give up Okra the cat? Why, when I lay down to sleep at night, the mice would gnaw at my feet if I didn't have Okra to chase them. That's just why I bought the cat."

"I've never seen a cat quite like that," said Aku as he stroked its smooth coat. Okraman and the cat rubbed noses. "He would be a fine companion for my family." By now Aku and Okraman had both completely forgotten about the vegetables they had set out to buy.

"Won't you sell it?" asked Aku.

"You can't afford it," said the man.

"How much does it cost?"

"It costs an asuanu-and-suru's weight in gold dust."

Aku plunged his hand into his sack. "Ha," he cried. "If that's what it costs, I'll take it!" He handed the gold dust to the man.

"Come Okra," he called, "come with me and Okraman." And the three of them trotted all the way home.

Aku and Okraman entered the hut with no plantains

or yams in sight. Then Okra the cat followed them in.

"Look at the cat that I bought, Mother!" cried Aku. "He always falls on his feet!"

"Oh Aku!" said Onyema," "another mouth to feed. And where are the vegetables?"

"The vegetables?" asked Aku, looking at Okraman. "The vegetables!" Then they remembered.

"One more," said Onyema again. "Now we are four, and what shall we eat? Aiee! It is what the Obosom said would happen. We are really in for it now if I do not go and get the yams and plantains myself."

So Onyema went and bought the vegetables herself.

AKU, OKRAMAN AND OKRA were treated as children in Onyema's household. Okra would leave his sleeping mat at night and curl up at the feet of Aku or Onyema. Okra also had his own dish for dinner just as the others did.

The three friends played together. They brought laughter and liveliness into Onyema's life. Sometimes they would pull her away from her chores to join them in a game around the pond in the compound.

Whenever the three visited Spider Ananse, he would give them a calabash full of ground nuts, palm nuts and kola nuts to take home to Onyema. On their way through the village, the children would chase after them singing:

Kwaku, Kwaku,
Fit Okra the cat,
Okraman and Aku
On one sleeping mat.

Onyema was proud of her large family, and she was grateful to the Abosom. On her visits of thanks to the Lesser God, Aku carried the offering of fruit, and Okra and Okraman followed.

Even so, with four in the family eating each mealtime, the food went faster and faster. The day came when Onyema mixed the last of the salt with the last of the fufu.

That evening, as they all sat to dinner, she said, "Listen children. We have fruits. We have nuts. But we are eating the last of the vegetables that I have stored."

Okra and Okraman were so busy licking the delicious fufu relish that they hardly looked up. Tomorrow, at that moment, meant nothing to them.

However Aku, between mouthfuls, spoke up and said, "Don't worry mother. Tomorrow Okra, Okraman and I will go to buy the food we need."

Onyema hesitated, thinking of the gold dust that had already been "burned." She remembered the proverb: "What a child wants he buys." But she had to admit that she too enjoyed having Okra and Okraman in the family.

So she said, "Aku, I've given you two chances, and I'll give you three. Promise not to forget what you set out to buy, for I have very little gold dust left."

Aku was sure he would remember this time. Besides he would have Okra and Okraman along to remind him.

The next morning Onyema weighed an asuasa's weight of gold dust and put the pouch in the sack with the fruits.

"Remember now, children," she said, "this gold dust is for salt, dried fish and vegetables only."

Onyema's last words soon faded in the excitement of the sights along the way. The dog and the cat bounded with such spirit that they soon forgot the where to, what for and why of their going.

Aku shared the fruit from his sack with them. He cast the seeds aside and looked to see if any of the last seeds had begun to sprout.

They were well on their way to the Edge-of-the-Sea Country market when they saw a youth carrying a brightly colored pigeon.

"What a beautiful bird!" exclaimed Aku as he stopped the youth. Okra and Okraman also came closer and admired the pigeon.

"Friend," said Aku, "I have seen pigeons flying in and out of my mother's garden, but I have never seen one like this. Where did you get it?"

"I caught it in a kingdom far away from here," said the youth. "I threw my net over it when it alighted on a bush. I keep this string tied to it's leg. It flies just so far then I pull it back. This amuses me, and I take it everywhere."

Aku touched the pigeon gently. Okra and Okraman licked its feathers. They completely forgot what they had set out to buy as they looked at the pigeon, then at each other. They had but one thought in mind.

Finally Aku said, "I would like to buy this bird."

"Ho! you could not afford it," said the youth. "This pigeon pleases me so much that I would not sell it for less than an asuasa's weight in gold dust."

"See here," said Aku holding out the gold dust. "Did you suppose that such a sum would stop me?"

He took the bird in his hands. Okra and Okraman leaped around him, happy to have this new friend for the family.

When they reached home, they all tried to talk at once. As soon as Onyema saw the bird, she knew the whole story even though not one clear word could be heard in the din.

Finally they quieted down, and Onyema said, "I see a pretty pigeon, but I don't see salt, dried fish and vegetables."

Salt! Dried fish! Vegetables!

They all remembered at once. The poor pigeon, sensing itself at the center of a calamity, closed it eyes and tucked its head under its wing.

"Aiee, now we are in for it," said Onyema. "This has turned out no better than before, except that the bird will eat like a bird. Still we'll need food. I see I cannot trust you to trade properly. I will have to go myself."

So Onyema took from the little she had left and went to buy the food herself.

The "burned" gold dust was soon forgotten as the pigeon became even more precious to the family than gold.

They named the bird Okera and catered to his special needs. The family could not bear to see the dear bird tied.

Aku said to Okera, "We will hold you by love or not at all," and he freed the bird.

Okera, the pigeon, had his own mat at meals and ate from a little clay dish. At night he slept on a sheltered

perch above Aku's sleeping mat.

After Aku's last adventure, whenever Onyema ran out of food, the whole household accompanied her to market. They made a lively troupe as they filed past the villagers, Onyema in the lead, followed by Aku, with the pigeon on his shoulder, while the dog and the cat trotted behind.

Now it was no longer just Onyema's garden and lily pond that the villagers admired, but her whole big family.

The little children joined the parade and chanted:

Kwaku, Kwaku,
We all parade with Aku,
The pigeon, dog and cat, too,
Onyema, what will you do?

Onyema knew quite well what she would do. If her children stopped too long over anything, she called "Hurry now! Catch up!"

And so, from that time on, the marketing that Onyema set out to do was always done.

The months passed.

One day Onyema weighed out the last of the gold dust. She called her family together and said, "Children, today we will buy our food in the marketplace with the last of our gold dust. After that, we will have to live on fruits, roots and the wild foods we can find in the forest."

She set off to market with Okra and Okraman. Aku stayed behind to gather dry branches and twigs for the fire. Okera, the pigeon, stayed with him.

When the others had gone Okera said, "Aku, you will soon run out of food because of the high price you paid for me. Listen to me now.

"In my kingdom I am a great chief. I was going on a journey when a stranger caught me and took me away. He kept me tied with a string until you bought me and freed me to become one of your family.

"You have been good to me. Now the time has come when I can help you. Take me back to my village and my people. There I have special powers. You will be rewarded."

Aku stared at Okera in surprise.

"You Okera, a great chief!" he exclaimed. He was confused. "You are planning to run away," he said.

"I have been free to do so and have not because I am bound to you by my word. That is why you must take me back. When we set out, tie a string to my leg. Try me, and you will not regret it."

When the others returned from the market, Aku said to them, "Tomorrow I am going on a journey to a distant place. Okera is homesick. I am returning him to his people, and we shall see what shall come of it."

The next day everyone awoke at dawn to bid Okera good-bye. Okra and Okraman had made a light necklace of bright seeds, which they gave Okera in parting. Onyema packed a small pouch of Okera's favorite food in the sack with Aku's fruits.

So they started on their journey, Aku holding the string as Okera perched on his shoulder.

For most of the morning, they traveled the known roads of Aku's country. Then they entered another world, the land beyond the villages that Aku knew. Here Okera pointed the way.

Late in the afternoon, Okera fluttered in excitement and flew down from Aku's shoulder. They had reached the outskirts of his kingdom. Just ahead, some children were crawling on the ground, rolling round seeds in a game of marbles.

When the children saw Okera they cried, "The King! The King!"

One of the boys ran to the palace crying, "The King! The King!"

He ran into the War Lord's chamber and cried, "O Korenti Chief, the King has returned!"

The Korenti Chief seized the boy.

"Why do you stir up our deep sorrow," he asked. "This is no game to play. You'll pay for this joke."

He took the boy before the Council of Chieftains. Just then another boy came rushing in. He ran to the chief guardian of the King's stool and said, "O Akwamu Chief! Our King has returned!"

"Now two boys tell the same tale," said the Akwamu Chief. "Perhaps they are not playing after all."

He addressed the chief treasurer and said, "Gyase Chief, go with these boys and see what this is all about."

The boys led the way. As soon as the Gyase Chief reached the place where the boys had been playing, he saw the pigeon surrounded by the children. He too recognized immediately the special markings of the bird and knew that it was the King.

The Gyase Chief rushed back to the palace to tell the chieftains that the story was true.

There was great excitement as the good news spread to the people. The Chiefs ordered the King's regalia and hammock to be brought out. They prepared at once to escort their leader back to the palace in style.

Aku untied the string that had bound Okera the pigeon. Standing free and on his own grounds, Okera's special powers returned to him.

No one noticed how or when Okera the pigeon resumed the form of Okera the King. All heads were turned towards the palace from which came the sounds of music and drumming.

The procession was on its way. The Queen Mother and the Chiefs were in the lead. Then came the elders and the King's servants and custodians, followed by the people of the tribes.

Aku was so caught up in the excitement of the procession that he forgot about his friend Okera the pigeon. It was only when Okera the King smiled at him from his hammock that Aku realized he had missed the transformation.

Okera the King motioned for his swordbearers to escort Aku to the palace.

There before all of his people the King told the whole story of his disappearance.

When the people heard of Aku's kindness to their King, they rose up to thank him. The Queen Mother presented Aku with a waterpot full of gold dust. The Chiefs each presented Aku with a waterpot full of gold dust.

The people asked Aku to stay and live among them. Aku thanked them but said that his family needed him and that he must return to his village in the morning.

The next day the pots of gold dust were strapped to a

donkey. When all was in readiness for Aku's departure, King Okera embraced him in farewell and said:

"Take this ring, Aku, my friend." He slipped a gold ring from his finger. "Guard it well. This ring has the power to give you whatever you desire."

OKRAMAN THE DOG and Okra the cat were playing in the forest near their home when they saw Aku coming down the road. They ran out to greet him with such welcoming shouts that Onyema ran to the gate to see what was happening.

Imagine her surprise when she saw her son returning, riding a donkey.

"Oh my!" she exclaimed. "He's given up the pigeon for a donkey. And pots of water in the bargain too, when we've got a well brimming over. Now we are really in for trouble!"

Onyema opened the gate as Aku rode into the compound. She loved her son and preferred facing any trouble with him to being alone. She threw her arms around him and said:

"Welcome, my son! I see you've brought lots of water for us."

Then nodding to Okra and Okraman she added:

"It must be special water, don't you think, or why would Aku have bothered? So let's all have a drink."

"Help yourself, Mother," said Aku.

Onyema opened the lid of a pot and dipped in. Aku laughed.

"Why, it's gold dust!" she cried.

One after the other, she looked into them all. From the donkey's back, Okra and Okraman peered in after her.

Each pot was filled with gleaming gold dust.

"Aku, my son, what a fortune!" she cried. "Where did you find it?"

Aku told the whole story of their friend Okera the King. Then he showed them the ring. Having seen pots of gold, the ring hardly seemed impressive.

Aku asked, "If you were given the choice between the pots of gold dust and this ring, which would you chose?"

They all laughed.

Onyema said, "I could buy many such rings with just one of those pots of gold dust."

Okra and Okraman nodded in agreement.

"Aha!" said Aku. "Then you would be fooled. I would not give up this ring for twice that weight in gold dust. It is a magic ring. Okera gave it to me. It has the power to grant wishes."

Aku's family was happy enough with the gold dust fortune! They were in no mood to argue about an insignificant ring.

Onyema prepared a great meal, and they feasted.

"Mother," said Aku, "today you do the chores with our help. Tomorrow you will be Queen Mother of the new village my ring will build for us. You will no longer have to work so hard."

"Queen Mother!" exclaimed Onyema. "Good, my son. Now get some rest. You've traveled a long way and you look tired. Tomorrow you'll feel better."

Aku tried to sleep, but he tossed and turned. Onyema worried that he might not be well, but he was simply impatient for the morning so that he could prove the worth of the ring. It was obvious to him that no one had believed his story of King Okera's magic ring.

At break of day Aku was up and on his way to the forest.

"Stay close to him, Okra and Okraman," Onyema whispered as she sent the dog and cat after her son. "He may need help."

Aku walked into the forest till he reached a wild, overgrown area. He cleared a small space, then slipped the ring off his finger and set it on the ground.

Aku closed his eyes and touching the ring he chanted:

> *Ring, now clear this land for me,*
> *Pile the brush and forest tree,*
> *Burn these heaps for fertile ground,*
> *Then build fine houses all around.*
> *Ring, bring people here to live*
> *And share the riches that I have.*
> *These separate wishes, linked as one*
> *Will prove your worth, when all is done.*

Aku opened his eyes and stood up. The ring set to work at once.

Okra and Okraman could hardly believe their eyes. They saw huge trees and bushes quietly uprooted. Flames that neither crackled nor smoked burned the piles to ashes. The ashes cooled instantly and fertilized the fields.

A new village sprang up right before their eyes. Onyema's compound was extended to include the fine houses of a palace. People were already seeding the ground.

They came out of their fields and houses to acclaim Aku as their chief. Onyema became Queen Mother, just as her son had said.

Aku thanked the ring and slipped it back on his finger. There he could guard it well. He was overjoyed with the new village. Okra and Okraman were his constant companions. Everywhere they went, they met the friendliness of the villagers.

Onyema was proud of her son and pleased with the good fortune that he had brought. She did not forget her offering of thanks to the Abosom.

The inhabitants of Chief Aku's village were kind people and good workers. They loved the land and they farmed well. If someone discovered a way to improve the crops, it was shared with the neighbors.

So Aku's village prospered by the people's own labor and resourcefulness.

WORD OF Chief Aku's remarkable village spread quickly to Spider Ananse's village and far beyond.

When Kwaku Ananse heard the news of Aku's fortune, he was astonished.

"How is that possible?" he thought. "A Spider-Story child is bound to get into trouble. It's been in such a rush to grow up that it mixes up everything. I became Aku's best friend to help him. It's only natural that Spider should help a Spider-Story child. But now I hear that he's a great chief of a prosperous village. I can't believe it! I will have to go and see for myself."

Spider Ananse set out for Aku's village. Soon, there it was before him, more wonderful than all the stories he had heard.

Kwaku Ananse paid his respects to the Queen Mother. He then sat and talked with Chief Aku. The wily Spider was so jealous of his friend's good fortune that he wailed:

> *O little mother's child,*
> *Child of good fortune.*
> *O little father's child,*
> *Child of success.*
> *You no longer care for Kwaku,*
> *You no longer look for Kwaku,*
> *Spider is forgotten,*
> *Alone and in distress.*

When Aku tried to assure Kwaku Ananse that he would always be dear to him, Ananse said:

"Easy enough to say! Yes, easy enough! Yet you won't even tell poor Ananse how you came by all this wealth."

Aku told Kwaku the whole story of his adventures. And Kwaku quivered with excitement when Aku told him about the magic ring.

"I must go now, I must go!" he cried hopping up. "I have a gift for you at home. I will go for it."

Spider Ananse was so anxious to get the ring away from Aku that he could hardly keep up with his plans or his feet. He tripped, tumbled and rolled all the way home, shouting:

The ring, the ring,
What a wonderful thing!

"Kwaku!" cried his niece Bintou, as he bounded into his hut. "Who's chasing you?"

"Oh Bintou," cried the breathless Ananse, "beautiful Bintou. You are just the one I need to help me."

Spider puffed and panted out the story of Aku's magic ring.

"I must have that ring, Bintou. I'm sending you with a gift to Chief Aku. Aku is fond of you. He will be happier to have you following him than his cat and dog. Watch carefully everything he does. He won't suspect anything. Do whatever he orders you to do. All the while you must secretly try to get that magic ring from him."

Kwaku Ananse gave Bintou his gift of palm wine to take to Chief Aku. Bintou balanced the pot on her head and went on her way.

The crafty Kwaku knew that Aku would be delighted to see Bintou.

"Ah Bintou," Aku greeted her as she arrived. "Thank you for bringing Kwaku's gift of palm wine. How thoughtful of your uncle."

Bintou's heart thumped when she saw the gold ring on Aku's finger. Aku held out his ringed hand to her and said:

"Come, we'll find my mother."

The Queen Mother was sitting by the lily pond. She rose to embrace Bintou.

"How lovely you have grown, Bintou," said Onyema. "Now that you are with us, you must stay for at least three days. There is so much in the new village that my son will want to show you."

For two days Aku and Bintou went everywhere together. Okra and Okraman often followed them. The villagers greeted Bintou as if she were their own daughter. She began to feel torn between her growing affection for Aku and his people and her loyalty to her uncle.

On the third day Bintou prepared to return to her village

with the presents she had been given. Her mission had failed, and she felt relieved. Aku had never removed the ring from his finger. She had found no way of taking it without his knowing. She arranged the presents in a large basket.

It was quite early, and Aku was also awake. He went down to the river to bathe.

Bintou walked toward the river, hoping to meet him on his way back and say good-bye. She walked quietly in the fresh dew and heard him still splashing in the water.

As she drew back not wishing to surprise him, she saw his clothes folded on a rock. A small bright object caught her eye. It glinted in the sun. It was the magic ring.

Now Bintou could not resist her curiosity about the ring. Aku was swimming far out in the river. He could not see her. She crept closer and touched the ring. For a moment she hesitated, then she remembered her uncle's care for her since she was a child. She took the ring and put it on her finger.

In her confusion, Bintou fled, forgetting the basket of presents. She avoided the well-traveled paths of the farmers and ran from the village without saying good-bye.

Aku came out of the water and dried in the
sun. He put on his clothes. Only then did he remember
the ring.

"Oh! It must have fallen when I took up my shirt," he
thought.

Aku searched the rock and the surrounding grasses,
without success. He decided to return to the compound
and get Okra and Okraman to help him.

They told him that Bintou had left in haste. Aku asked
if there had been a message from her uncle. No one knew.
Aku realized in surprise that he felt the sudden loss of
Bintou even more than the loss of the magic ring.

As soon as Spider Ananse laid his hands on the ring, he
clapped and danced around Bintou. He kissed her and
cried:

"I'm the happiest Spider south of the River Niger! Ring,
build me a town! Bigger! Bigger! Even bigger than Aku's
town."

The ring worked hard for Spider till it had built the
biggest town of all the kingdoms known around.

In the center of his compound Spider Ananse had a
sound hut built. The outer walls were thick and smooth as
butter, without a seam. No lock or door was to be seen.
A secret entrance was hidden nearby between the roots of

a tree. It led through a tunnel that came up in the floor of the hut. No one but Spider Ananse knew how to enter.

Spider didn't dare wear the ring. He sat inside the hut rubbing his treasure till it gleamed. He sang to himself:

> *O ring, ring, ring,*
> *You wonderful thing!*

Then Spider thought of an ingenious scheme for hiding the ring and set to work.

Kwaku began by crafting a huge box that stood in the center of the hut. Into this box, Spider fit another box.

Spider worked carefully, fashioning box within box. Each lid locked by a tricky latch that took two taps to trip. Within this nest of boxes nestled the smallest box of all, made of African ironwood. Here Spider hid the ring.

Spider Ananse stood back and admired his boxes. He sang out with pride:

"What a mighty hiding place for the magic ring! Who would guess that it takes two taps, three raps and a kick to trip this last latch? Tee aha hee!

Now Spider Ananse was set. He had everything he wished for, and the ring was secure. He rushed about the town with a train of attendants, giving orders and cancelling engagements. He had more affairs to handle now than when he had managed nine webs.

Kwaku Ananse rewarded his neice with fine clothes of silk and gold. She was dressed like a princess and had fan bearers to wait upon her. However Bintou didn't enjoy the attention she now received as much as the attention she had received in Chief Aku's village.

"Uncle," said Bintou, "now that we have everything we wish, let me return the ring to Aku.

"What!" cried her uncle. "The ring, the ring, that marvelous thing! And have Aku build a town larger than my own? Never!"

Meanwhile, Aku, Okra the cat and Okraman the dog searched for the ring. They combed the grasses by the stream, but the ring could not be found.

Onyema said to her son:

"Aku, take an offering and consult the Obosom who has been so good to us. Perhaps the Obosom will help you find the ring."

Aku wasted no time. Off he went with Okra and Okraman trotting beside him. When the offering had been presented, the Obosom spoke:

> *While you swam*
> *Bintou came.*
> *She took the ring*
> *And hurried home.*
>
> *Spider wished for a town*
> *Once the ring was his own,*
> *A town larger than yours,*
> *The ring built one.*
>
> *Now the ring is tucked*
> *In the center box*
> *Housed in a hut*
> *Without doors or locks.*
>
> *Send Okraman the dog*
> *With Okra the cat*
> *To win back the ring*
> *And determine their fate.*

Okra and Okraman couldn't understand what the ring had to do with their fate, but they were eager to go in search of it.

Despite all of his precautions, Spider Ananse was still not sure that the magic ring was secure. Perhaps news of his great town had reached Aku by now. What would Aku plan to do to get back his ring?

Spider Ananse prepared an offering and consulted his Obosom for instructions.

Kwaku listened carefully to the cryptic stanzas of the Obosom:

> *Kwaku, great uncle*
> *Hear what I say,*
> *Paws and jaws*
> *Are on the way.*
>
> *Jaws and paws*
> *Will search the town*
> *And seize the hole*
> *That gold goes round.*
>
> *Riddle my words,*
> *Be cautious! Take care!*
> *Or awaken to find*
> *Your middle box bare.*

Spider Ananse trembled with excitement when he heard the Obosom. Nothing pleased him more than a good riddle. His mind was fired at once to decipher the Obosom's words.

"Paws," he pondered. "That must mean Okra the cat, for 'jaws' is certainly Okraman the dog. 'Paws,' cat. 'Jaws,' dog.

"They are coming to 'seize the hole that gold goes round!' I've got it! I've got it! That means the magic ring! And 'the middle box bare' means they plan to take the ring away from me.

"So Aku is planning to send the cat and the dog to steal back the ring! They'll never get into the hut without doors or open boxes with trick latches. Tee hee aha! Tee hee aha hee!

"Well, I'll be ready for them anyway. I'll see to it that they never even reach the village."

Spider Ananse ran back to his compound.

"Bintou, Bintou," he called. "Quick! There's no time to lose. I've just discovered that Aku plans to send Okra and Okraman to get back the ring, and I plan to stop them.

"Listen, I'll line the path to our village with pieces of drugged meat. Run for the medicine, Bintou, while I cut up the meat."

Bintou ran for the medicine that her uncle ordered, but she stopped just long enough to send a messenger to warn

Aku of Kwaku's plans.

Spider churned the choice chunks of lamb in a pot. He chuckled over his plan. Bintou returned and drenched the meat with the medicine.

"Now, Bintou," said Kwaku, "take one handle of this pot! We must put the meat along the path before Okra and Okraman get here."

Together they lugged the pot to the path and placed the pieces of meat in the way.

While Spider Ananse stirred his pot and laid his trap, Aku sat with Okra the cat and Okraman the dog.

"Okra and Okraman," said Aku, "since I brought you to my mother's house, you have been close friends. Now I need your help. You can prove that I did a good thing when I bought you.

"Spider Ananse has stolen the magic ring that belongs to me. He's locked it tightly in the center box of a nest of boxes. The Obosom also said that these boxes are hidden in a hut without doors.

"I cannot go on this adventure myself. Therefore, I have chosen you, above all others in the kingdom, to win back the ring. I know I can trust you, for that is the reason I bought you."

Okra and Okraman were eager to start. Just then Bintou's messenger entered the gate to the court and gave Aku the message.

Aku thanked the messenger and said: "Tell Bintou that I will send for her as soon as the ring is recovered."

Aku dismissed the messenger and turned to Okra and Okraman.

"You heard the news," he said. "Kwaku has put drugged meat on the path to the hut where the magic ring is hidden. When you reach there, don't touch the meat! Jump over it!"

"I heard," said Okraman, "but did Okra hear through the fuzz in his ears?"

"Fuzz doesn't make a buzz of a difference," answered Okra. "I heard every word, in spite of the loud sniffling of one who goes with his nose sniffing the ground."

"Kaou, Kao!" barked Okraman, "when I sniff out the ring, you'll sing sweeter things."

"Maou, meow!" mewed Okra. "If it's by a nose that the ring's to be found, then I'll wear one in my nose."

"Enough!" said Aku. "If you two don't work together on this venture, I'll end up without the ring, and without Bintou."

They stopped quarreling. Neither wanted that to happen. So Okra the cat and Okraman the dog set off on their adventure together.

THEY STARTED out proudly. Each was certain he would distinguish himself in the quest for the ring. Okraman was loud in his boasts. Okra remembered Aku's words and, to avoid quarreling, went along in silence.

At last they reached the path leading to Spider Ananse's village. Okraman sniffed the meat at a distance. He no sooner saw the tempting morsels than his boasts turned to ghosts.

"Okra, cat," said Okraman," I can't go another step. I have an awful pain in my stomach . . . and a cramp in my legs and a twitch in my left eye and a lump in my tail."

"Don't fail me now," said Okra. "We're in this together. The business on hand is very important."

"So is my health," said Okraman. "Let me lie here until the pain passes. Then I'll catch up with you and get the ring."

As soon as Okra had disappeared from sight, Okraman snatched the meat and gulped it down. He ate every bit of it and said:

"Hmm, yum, now I feel fit for the search."

Okraman started after Okra, but the drug soon took effect. He had only gone a few steps when he collapsed in a heap. He lay down in the path, fast asleep.

Okra the cat reached Spider Ananse's hut. He circled it several times, but there was no way to enter through the smooth, thick walls.

Just then a pigeon flew onto the roof of the hut. He picked a spot and pecked the thatch. Then the pigeon pulled some straw and flew off with it in its beak.

Okra leaped to the roof and crept to the spot where the pigeon had plucked a space. There was a small opening in the thatch, just big enough for Okra to squeeze through.

Okra crouched on the rafters. A dim light filtered through the thatch. All was quiet within.

Okra dropped to the ground and tried the latch of the large box. The lock held fast. Okra wondered:

"How will I get through to the magic ring if I can't even

open the outer box?"

Just then Okra heard a sound. He quickly returned to his place on the rafters and watched carefully to see who would enter.

Okra saw the earth spilling from the wall. Suddenly mouse pushed through the hole he had made and ran into the hut. When mouse passed directly beneath him, Okra dropped, blam! right on mouse's head.

"Squeak, squeak, squeak, squeak," cried mouse. "Get off my head. Don't hurt me!"

"Hurt you? I'm going to eat you!" said Okra.

"Squeak, squeak! Please don't eat me," said mouse.

"Why not?" asked Okra. "What can you do for me?"

"What do you want?" asked mouse. "Perhaps I can help you."

"I want what belongs to my friend." said Okra. "Spider Ananse has stolen Chief Aku's ring and hidden it in these boxes. Get me the ring, and I will let you go."

"I can do that," said mouse. "But first you must free me."

"Aha!" said Okra the cat. "Mouse tricks! What will keep you from bolting once I let go of you?"

"I promise not to run away," said mouse.

"Promises spoken are easily broken," said Okra, "but a tough string's another thing."

"Then fasten a string around my waist," said mouse.

Okra tied a string around mouse's waist. Mouse went

to work with his sharp teeth. He gnawed until he made a hole through the outer box. Then he nibbled through the next box, chewed through the next and bit through the next.

Finally, mouse reached the smallest box of all, the ironwood box containing the magic ring. Mouse gnawed, nibbled, chewed and bit his way through that tough box.

Mouse took the ring and ran back through the narrow passage he'd made. Okra the cat was so delighted to have the ring that he kissed Mouse and untied the string.

Mouse squealed when kissed by the cat. He believed that was the taste before the first bite, a sign of the end. When the string fell, he squeaked his thanks and streaked off without looking behind.

NOW THAT he had the ring, Okra was quick to leave the hut through the hole in the thatched roof. He reached the path and found Okraman stretched out in the way, fast asleep.

"Okraman, Okraman," he called as he shook the dog awake. "Did your pains pass?"

"Nothing bothers me now," said groggy Okraman. "Did you get the ring?"

"Where's the meat we were warned not to touch?" asked Okra.

"How should I know?" answered Okraman. "Perhaps as I slept the pain off, the villagers came and took it. Did you get the ring?"

"You look much fatter than when I left you," said the cat. "Are you sure you didn't touch the meat?"

"Why keep harping on that?" said the dog irritably. "I've told you all I know. Now tell me, did you get the ring?"

"Yes," said Okra, "and we'd better leave before Spider Ananse finds out. See? Here it is!"

"Good," said Okraman the dog. "I knew we could do it."

They ran from Spider's village and came to a river. The river was in flood.

"Okra," said Okraman, "the water is very deep and the current is swift. You know you hate the water and cross by walking on the bottom.

"I love the water and cross by swimming on the surface.

Let me carry the ring in my jaws. I will paddle across with my head in the air. The ring will be dry and safe with me."

"That's true," said the cat. He put the ring in Okraman's mouth.

They both jumped into the river and started for the other side. Okra crossed quickly on the bottom and came out on the opposite shore.

Okraman was proud to have the magic ring in his mouth. He paddled importantly. By midstream, the swift current caught him.

Okraman was so stuffed that he had trouble staying afloat. He became annoyed with his care in breathing and forgot all about the ring in his mouth. He gasped for breath, and the ring fell into the water.

"That's that!" said the dog. "The ring's lost, but I'm not. I can breathe much better now."

Okraman flopped and paddled and thrashed till at last he crawled up on the shore. Okra sat waiting.

"What took you so long? This is no time to play in the water," said Okra. "We must hurry. Give me the ring!"

"That ring was almost the death of me," complained Okraman. "How did you expect me to breathe with a ring in my mouth? I opened my mouth to breathe, and the ring fell out."

"What?" cried Okra the cat. "Aku will not be pleased to hear that. He trusted us to bring back the ring."

"And ourselves too," said the Dog! "I could have drowned."

The cat leaped back into the water. The ring was not there, but a large fish was passing. Okra snatched it.

"Let me go! Let me go!" cried the fish. "You're hurting me."

"Do as I say, or you'll be in more trouble," said Okra. "My friend's ring has fallen into this river, and if you don't give it back to me, I'll eat you!"

The fish shivered and said, "Take me to the riverbank, and I will give you what belongs to you."

Okra hauled the fish to the shore and set the fish on the riverbank. The fish coughed up the ring.

"Thank you, friend fish," said Okra.

He took the ring and tossed the fish back into the river. The fish flicked its tail on the surface of the water, then sank from sight.

"Did you get the ring back?" asked Okraman.

Okra showed Okraman the magic ring.

"Listen, dear cat," said Okraman, "you know that we have always shared things equally. Let's keep it that way. Don't tell Aku or Onyema what I did, and we'll continue to live together as we always have."

Okra the cat, however, had put the ring in his mouth and refused to speak. He made no promises. He remained silent all the way home.

Some of the village boys saw Okra and Okraman returning. They ran to tell their Chief. Aku called out the drummers, and there was a great welcoming procession for the
cat and the dog.

While Okra and Okraman were away, everyone had
learned of their important mission. The villagers had been
on the lookout for the return of Okra and Okraman.

When the procession arrived at Chief Aku's court, Okra
the cat took the magic ring and put it on Aku's finger.

The villagers cheered and danced to the lively beat of
the drummers. Then they took their places to listen to the
tale of the magic ring's return.

Okraman the dog didn't dare begin. He drew back in silence.

Okra the cat stepped forward. He took a little harp from one of the court musicians, tuned the strings and began to sing the story of his adventure:

Queen Mother, Chief Aku,
Villagers all,
Hear the long tale,
Though pared to the core,
That I've lived to tell.
The recent adventure
Of the dog and the cat.

It will illustrate that
One's own behavior
Determines his fate.
I, Okra, now sing
Of the Quest for the Ring.

We came to the meat
We were told not to eat,
Okraman played sick,
I saw through the trick,
He lay down
I went on.

As soon as I'd gone,
He gulped all
The meat, then toppled
and fell asleep.

I came to the hut
That Spider had shut
Without latch or lock.
I saw pigeon remove
A straw from above.
I sprang to the roof
And crawled through the groove
In the thatch
On the house.
I came out of a crouch
And fell upon mouse
Before he knew why.

Mouse has a way,
Without knock or key,
Of gaining entry.
He nibbles until
There's no obstacle.
Mouse walks where he will.

I made a bargain.
In exchange for his life
He'd bring me the ring.
So for me now
Mouse gnawed a door through
The tightly shut boxes,
Avoiding the latches,
And came to the ring.

I held mouse by a string
Till I saw the deed done.
Mouse won his freedom,
And I started for home.
I stopped and I shook
The dog. He awoke
And took Aku's prize
Where the wide river rose.

On the surface dog tossed,
On the bottom I crossed
And quickly passed over.
Okraman crossed after
Puffing. He thrashed
In the water.

63

He was so stuffed
He gasped in midstream
And lost the ring.
I jumped back in haste
When I learned of this,
And caught the fish
That swallowed the ring.
I threatened to sup
On his silvery bones
If he didn't give up
What I'd rightly won.

Fish coughed up the ring.
I held the prize fast.
This was the last
Of the chances I'd take
For Okraman's sake.
It would not do
For me to let go
Of the magic ring
Till I brought it to you.

Okraman now wishes
That we share the praises
Of our adventure
Though he was a failure.

The Obosom had said
We'd determine our fate
And prove Aku's trust
By our acts on this quest.

Here I let my song rest.
I've sung as I must.
You will do what is just.
I've sung what is so
All the way through;
My tale is now over.

Long live the Queen Mother.
All power to you
Dear Brother, Aku.

Okra the cat finished his recital and returned the harp. Chief Aku gave the signal for the drummers and other instrumentalists to play their thanks to Okra the cat. The audience danced and chanted:

Praise be to Okra the cat.
He brought back the magic ring.
Praises to the bright cat
Who went conquering.
Praise to the cat, sing!

Okraman the dog had nothing to say after the Cat's epic chant. He tucked his tail between his legs and hung his head in shame.

After the "Praise Song to Okra the Cat," the villagers turned towards Okraman the dog. Words could not describe their disappointment in him so they shouted:

> *Eee, yee! Eee, yee!*
> *The dog is worthless,*
> *Eee, yee! Eee, yee!*
> *But cat is priceless,*
> *Eee, yee!*

Chief Aku ordered a feast to celebrate the return of the magic ring. He sent for Bintou. She sat in the place of honor between him and the Queen Mother.

Bintou expected harsh words for what she had done, but Spider's antics were well known and her loyalty to her uncle was understood by all. The villagers also knew that Chief Aku planned to marry Bintou, and then there would be no question of her loyalty. She was treated with kindness.

When the feast was prepared and all had gathered, Chief Aku spoke:

"Everyone, hear what I say. My friend Okra the cat, whose deeds were so great, shall share all I have. No mat-

2 THE CAT AND THE DOG

ter what I am eating, I will take some of it, break it and place it in your little dish, Okra. Whatever mat I sleep upon, you may choose the part you wish and lie upon it with me."

The villagers cheered their approval:

> *Praise be to Okra the cat.*
> *Praises to the bright cat.*
> *Praise to the cat,*
> *The cat!*

Then Chief Aku continued:

"As for Okraman the dog, whose deeds were so shameful, your food will be leftovers, tossed on the ground. When the chilly night winds come, you will lie outdoors on the smouldering embers of the dead fire.

"People will remember your disgrace. They will whip you with switches when you get in their way."

FROM THAT time on, to this day, you will always see the Cat lying on the best mat in house or hut. Cat will not touch food cast down on the ground. His manners are fine. He is an aristocrat. Cat must be served on a plate or he will not eat.

As for the Dog, from that day to this, you will always see him sleeping in the courtyard, trying to keep warm on the dead ashes of the day's fire.

Dog will gulp anything down that's thrown to him. His manners are gross. He eats from the ground. When he's beaten for being underfoot, you'll hear him yelp:

"Kaou kao! Kaou kao!"

SO IT IS that the fate of the Dog and the Cat was set in the time of Onyema's Spider-Story Child. The adventures of Aku are like the nest of boxes that Spider Ananse built.

One adventure opens into another. So it goes until we reach the final adventure. This adventure is like the middle box that held the magic ring, for this last story holds the key to why it is that we always see the Cat lying on a velvet cushion, while the Dog sleeps among the ashes.

I've told the tale through. You may take some as true and go with it. Yet, I'll expect a share of what's told, born out of the old.

Return it on night winds, when rushes bow low below breezes blowing on and over Onyema's lily pond. Hear the rustling tones! What seemed the plant noises of rushes are voices whispering new adventures of Aku. Listen!

This is my story. Whether it be bitter or whether it be sweet, praise me for that and the telling of it. Take some of it elsewhere and as you go, let the rest come back home to me.